TEMPTING FATE
A LOVE IN EDEN SHORT

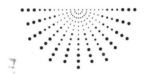

SLOANE KENNEDY

Tempting Fate is a work of fiction. Names, characters, businesses, places, events and incidents are either the products of the author's imagination or used in a fictitious manner. Any resemblance to actual persons, living or dead, or actual events is purely coincidental.

Copyright © 2019 by Sloane Kennedy

Published in the United States by Sloane Kennedy.

All rights reserved. This book or any portion thereof may not be reproduced or used in any manner whatsoever without the express written permission of the publisher except for the use of brief quotations in a book review.

Cover Image: © Wander Aguiar

Cover Design: © Cate Ashwood Designs

Copyediting by Courtney Bassett

ISBN: 9781661981099

AUTHOR NOTE

Please note that this story was previously published as part of a charity anthology so it was intended to be a certain length. Although it is a complete story with an HEA, if you don't care for short stories, Jackson and Travis's tale may not be for you.

CHAPTER 1

TRAVIS

"Come on, Jackson, get a move on!" I shouted the second I walked into the room. Not surprisingly, I was rewarded with a volley of swear words coming from the direction of the bathroom. Well, they weren't actually real swear words. I supposed that was what happened when you had a kid.

I'd only known Jackson a few years, but the few times I'd heard him let loose on some guy because he'd been too rough with a horse or cow, I'd been stunned by the older ranch hand's show of temper. There had been no holding back the swear words in *those* particular cases. Hell, there'd even been a time or two when he'd let his fists fly. We might've worked on a cattle ranch where the animals' fates were undeniable, but unlike a lot of the men in our business, Jackson believed every living thing, whether it had hooves, paws, wings or scales, deserved respect and kindness. It was what had first drawn me to the man when I'd started at Broken Tree Ranch, especially since I'd grown up believing men had to be men and that meant using one's fists instead of their words to get their point across.

I heard the shower come on and shook my head. Jackson Doyle was a gentle soul when it came to delivering a calf or patching up one of the ranch's horses, but he sucked at being on time for anything. In that sense, he was as bad as all the women I'd ever dated put together.

"*Dated...* right Travis," I murmured to myself. Dated was a generous term for the kinds of relationships I'd been having with women pretty much from the moment I'd figured out how fond of them my dick was.

I strode across the small room which consisted of a bed, loveseat, and a few small kitchen appliances and practically stomped into the bathroom.

"You've got two minutes," I declared as I ripped the shower curtain back. "I finally got Brandy to agree to meet me—" I began to say, but my words got stuck in my throat as my eyes fell on Jackson. He was in the midst of washing his semi-hard dick and something about the sight of his hand on his own junk had me feeling like cotton had been shoved into my mouth and the frogs I'd been so fond of catching as a kid were jumping around in my belly.

"Jesus, Travis," Jackson snapped as he jerked back in surprise. I told myself to look up, but my eyes were glued to his wet, soapy cock. It was only when he jerked the shower curtain closed that whatever spell had fallen over me broke. I felt hot and cold all over as Jackson yelled, "I'll be out in five!"

I might have grumbled some kind of response, but I wasn't sure as I turned and practically fled the bathroom. My skin went from hot and cold to all hot, and I ended up reaching to see if my forehead was sweating because it sure as hell felt like I was feverish.

What the hell is wrong with me?

I found myself circling Jackson's living space as I tried to catch my breath. The image of water sliding over his naked body refused to leave my brain, so I forced myself to focus on the sparse room instead. I'd been in the place hundreds of times, since it was usually me who was making sure Jackson was up every morning so that he wouldn't be late for the day's assignments at breakfast. Our boss, Mac, ran a tight ship, or in our case, a tight ranch. But we were well compensated for the long, hard hours we put in. Our pay was good, but unlike most of the ranches in the area, the senior hands at Broken Tree had the added perk of having their own living space. Jackson and I, along with four other hands, shared a small house on the ranch's property. The newer ranch hands were consigned to living in a bunkhouse where they didn't have as much privacy.

While my room tended to have a more cluttered look, Jackson's was neat and tidy and the only decorations were pictures of his ex-wife and kid. Those were by his bed. I found myself heading in that direction. I wasn't sure why I was so drawn to the photographs. Maybe because it was still so hard to fathom that Jackson had once been a family man with a pretty young wife and a son. Jackson was such a quiet, distant man around most people that I struggled to envision him coming home from work each day and greeting a wife and child. But at the same time, I knew he was nothing like my own father, who'd had a passel of kids and had ignored them all in favor of a case of beer each night.

I'd always wondered why Jackson was no longer married. He'd never really told me why he and Jolene had broken up after seventeen years of marriage, but as I studied the pictures, I couldn't help but once again wonder what had gone wrong between them. Jackson clearly loved being a dad and he and Jolene seemed to get along well so it didn't really make sense to me why their marriage had ended.

I set the pictures back down on the nightstand and was about to get up when I noticed a laptop sitting open on Jackson's bed. I told myself not to snoop, but I couldn't really help it I hadn't known the man even had a laptop, let alone actually used it. It'd taken me years just to get him to upgrade his flip phone to a smart phone so that he could video chat with his kid.

His computer was open to his email program. Guilt for even looking at that much had me starting to turn away when my eyes suddenly caught on a few words in bold.

Thank you, your ad has been successfully posted.

I felt my heart jump into my throat at the word "ad." Was Jackson considering leaving Broken Tree Ranch? Maybe that was why he had the laptop... so he could hunt for jobs. The idea of him leaving the ranch, or worse, the town of Eden altogether, had my breathing increasing again. It was all I could do not to stride into the bathroom and demand an explanation.

Take a breath, Travis.

They were Jackson's words.

Ones he often spoke to me when I'd get too worked up about something. He always said them to me in the calmest of voices and he usually put his hand on my shoulder and kept it there until I could get control of myself again. The strangest things had a way of setting me off and bringing back the ugliness of my childhood, but Jackson was always there to guide me back to the present. And he'd managed to do it in a way that none of the other hands, or Mac himself, ever saw.

Everyone else viewed me as the young hothead who liked taking risks and pushing boundaries. I was always the first one to jump off the cliff and into the murky depths without knowing what was beneath the choppy waters, but it wasn't for the reasons that everyone thought. Only Jackson knew that it was fear that drove me to the edge of that cliff, not excitement. I didn't know why, but he'd always covered for me. What was stranger, though, was that we never talked about it. I knew he knew how messed up I really was, but I hid from him as surely as I did from everyone else. Yet, when I was in the midst of having one of my moments where my temper got the best of me or it was fear rather than passion that drove my responses, Jackson was the one talking me down and reminding me to breathe.

I did just that as I pulled the laptop closer.

Jackson wasn't going anywhere.

I'd make sure of that.

Even if I had to talk to Mac myself about a pay raise for Jackson or I had to beg Jolene not to move their kid somewhere that would force Jackson to follow, the man was staying put. I didn't care how selfish I was being. I reasoned that it was what was best for Jackson, not me.

But as I started reading the ad in the bottom half of the email, my worry was replaced by shock. When I finished reading it, I started all over again just to be sure I'd read it right the first time.

We bonded over a screw... of the nuts and bolt variety.

In search of the guy I met at Delaney's Hardware in Casper.

You asked for my number, but I didn't give it to you.
Hoping fate will give me a second chance.
Remember the cabin I mentioned? Meet me there next weekend.
I'm ready for more now.

All I could do was stare at the short little sentences as I tried to make sense of what they meant.

Disbelief reverberated through me and I found myself slamming the laptop shut.

"He's gay," I whispered to myself because if I didn't say it out loud, I knew my brain would never be able to process it.

Jackson was gay. He was gay and he'd kept it from me.

The sense of betrayal was keen.

I began pacing back and forth by the bed, eyeing the laptop like it was the source of all evil. I wanted to kick myself for having even looked at the damn thing in the first place. Not only was I an asshole for invading Jackson's privacy, but I was an even bigger asshole for being so pissed... and not really knowing why. My fists were clenched at my sides and it took everything in me not to punch a hole in the wall.

I started for the bathroom, intending to demand that Jackson tell me why he'd kept such a big secret from me, when my eyes once again fell on the laptop.

It was like things were in slow motion because even as I continued to make my way to the bathroom for the mother of all confrontations, the rest of the ad sunk in.

I came to an abrupt stop when I realized that the ad was, in fact, an *ad*. As in a *personals* ad. As in a *Jackson-wants-to-get-laid* kind of ad.

What other reason would there be to place an ad to find a guy he'd already met and who he was inviting to the little cabin he'd inherited from his grandfather. The little cabin that only *he and I* had ever gone to before. Not even his wife had been in the remotely located, rustic hunting cabin.

It was all too much. The secret he'd been hiding, the stranger he was inviting to the place that I'd always thought of as being a little bit mine, the fact that he'd seen so much of who I really was but had never given me a glimpse into that part of his life...

This time, I was unable to stop myself from slamming my fist into the wall.

I wanted to scream and rage. I wanted to grab Jackson and ask him what the hell he'd been thinking. Not only was he risking himself by exposing who he was in our small Wyoming town that wasn't exactly liberal, but he was inviting a virtual stranger into his life and potentially his bed. Visions of some guy holding Jackson down as he hurt him had me seeing red and for the second time, I slammed my fist into the wall, only this time I went straight through the drywall.

"What the—" I heard Jackson say at the same time that the bathroom door flew open. "Jesus, Travis," he snapped, much like he had when I'd interrupted his shower, but his words quickly died off when his eyes fell to my hand.

He was in front of me a second later and there was no hesitation in his touch as he grabbed my hand and began examining it. I knew there was probably supposed to be pain considering my knuckles were bruised and bloodied, but I didn't feel any of it. I was still stuck on the image of Jackson being pinned to a bed with some sick fuck holding him down.

Though Jackson was only in his mid-thirties and fit from working long days on the ranch, he wasn't a particularly large guy. I probably outweighed him by a good fifty pounds. While I came from a family who knew how to throw a punch, Jackson was the son of a minister. While he might get worked up about some injustice being done to one of the cows, horses or dogs that called the ranch home and maybe even throw a punch or two, I wasn't sure he knew the first thing about defending himself.

"What the hell happened?" Jackson asked as he took my hand and began leading me to the small utility sink in the space that was technically his kitchen. His eyes drifted back to the hole I'd left in the wall.

I waited for him to grill me about it, but his attention quickly returned to the back of my hand as he carefully began washing the blood from it. It wasn't until that moment that I realized he was wearing only a towel around his hips and that water was dripping down his body. His hair was soaking wet and looked like it had flecks of shampoo still in it. I had no idea why, but I found myself pulling in deep breaths in the hopes that I could smell it.

"Are you all right?" Jackson asked gently when he turned off the water and began wrapping a dish towel around my fingers.

No, I wasn't. I really wasn't. But that wasn't what I said.

"Sorry, just got... lost in my thoughts, I guess," I mumbled.

Anyone else on the ranch would've asked what I was talking about, but not Jackson. His fingers carefully wrapped around my hand to hold the towel in place. His eyes were full of understanding. "Do you want to talk about it?"

I shook my head. "No," I said truthfully.

The absolute *last* thing I wanted to do was talk about it. Even if the "it" he was talking about wasn't the "it" I was thinking about. It just made me more of a dick to let him believe I was upset about a memory from when my dad had knocked me around.

Jackson didn't seem surprised by my reluctance. He held onto my hand for a moment longer before checking the wound. I used that opportunity to study him in more detail. His dark hair was a little shorter than mine, but I didn't see any gray in it. I'd seen him shirtless often enough, but I'd somehow missed the fact that he was quite muscular. He was clean-shaven but there was a bit of a five o'clock shadow happening. His lips were more pink than red and for some reason my mind was hung up on the fact that I couldn't describe them in any other way besides *plump*.

It was the most ridiculous way to think of a man's mouth. Not to mention I shouldn't even be thinking of a man's mouth in the first place.

That same sense of agitation that had driven my fist through the wall came back and it was all I could do not to rip my hand free of Jackson's and ask him what the fuck he was thinking with that stupid ad. I almost ended up glancing at the hated laptop but somehow managed to keep my eyes on him. My skin felt warm and tingly where he was touching it and I wondered why.

Probably just a delayed pain response, I told myself.

"Let me go get a bandage," Jackson said softly as his eyes lifted to mine. The way he was looking at me made it feel like I'd been punched in the gut. I told myself it was the sense of betrayal that was making me feel breathless and nothing else.

"It's fine," I snapped as I pulled my hand from his. The strange tingling sensation stopped.

What the fuck?

"I'll fix the wall," I bit out. I swore that Jackson actually looked hurt. He glanced over his shoulder at the wall and then shook his head.

"Don't worry about it," he said.

I felt like an even bigger asshole for my behavior and that just made me more confused. I knew I should apologize but all I could think about was that goddamn ad.

I'm ready for more now.

What exactly was he ready for? To fuck a guy? To do more than that? I wanted to yell at him that he couldn't be *out* in a town like Eden. Hell, most of Wyoming wouldn't accept him. Not only would he be putting his job at risk, his very life could be at stake.

That's not what has you upset.

I told the voice in my head to shove it and took a step back from Jackson. His expression fell and he turned on his heel. "I'll be out in a minute," he said. "Wouldn't want you to keep Brandy waiting," he added, his voice full of irritation.

It took me a good twenty seconds to remember who the hell Brandy was. Ten minutes ago she'd been the woman I'd been chasing for weeks… not for a date, but for some harmless fun for one night. Now I just wanted to blow the woman off so that I could figure out how to tell Jackson he was making a terrible mistake.

I began pacing the room again, the throbbing in my hand starting to become more obvious. But the pain helped keep me grounded. Unfortunately, it wasn't exactly helpful because as I worked to dismiss the idea of Jackson being hurt by some guy, I started to wonder about whoever the nameless, faceless man was that he was trying to find.

What if it turned into something? What if the "more" he was

talking about really happened? The image I'd had earlier of Jackson being held down by his would-be assailant shifted to one of him clinging to a hard body that was covering his. I didn't even really understand the logistics of it, but in my head I saw Jackson lying beneath the man he was so eager to find. Jackson's head was thrown back and his arms were wrapped around the guy's naked back. Their mouths were fused together and there was sweat clinging to Jackson's body. The moans that were falling from his lips were...

"Fuck," I breathed as my own body reacted to the vision in my head.

What the hell was wrong with me? Why was I thinking about Jackson and his would-be lover? It was absolutely none of my business. He'd made it so by not telling me about any of it.

Between the emotions that were consuming me and my body reacting physically to the image I couldn't get out of my head, I felt like a raw, exposed nerve. I was dimly aware of the shower shutting off. I tried to focus on the fact that it meant that I'd get to see Brandy soon—that I'd be able to grab her and drag her to the bathroom in the back of the shitty bar we were going to. She wasn't exactly discriminating when it came to sex in public places. I knew that because I'd seen her and her boyfriend going at it in his truck as well as the alley behind the hair salon where she worked.

But none of my thoughts were about fucking Brandy against the stall in the bathroom or having her on her knees in front of me, expertly taking me to the back of her throat.

My eyes shifted to the laptop on Jackson's bed. Before I even knew what I was doing, I was sitting in front of it and opening it back up. Thankfully, Jackson hadn't thought to secure the laptop with a password, so it opened right back up to the email it'd been on. I scanned the whole thing again. The hosting site was something called Heart2-Heart. I saw some kind of tagline relating to the LGBTQ community, but my eyes lingered on the line beneath the ad itself.

I could hear movement on the other side of the wall and knew I had just minutes to act. I ignored my conscience, which repeatedly told me to get up and walk away from the computer, and I ignored what it meant that I was doing what I was doing. In fact, I ignored everything in my head *except* for the one word that I kept repeating to myself as I imagined Jackson making love to the man he'd asked fate to give him a second chance at being with.

No.

It was only when the confirmation email came through that the ad had been deleted that I finally felt the tiniest measure of relief. It took only a few more seconds to find and delete all of the website's emails from Jackson's inbox. When I went to the website itself, I saw that Jackson already had several responses. That just stiffened my resolve and I worked quickly to delete his account in its entirety. My fingers were numb by the time I was done and when Jackson came out of the bathroom, I was back to pacing and trying to work up the nerve to tell him what I'd just done. But then I saw the bandage in his hand and when he warned me not to argue with him as he started fixing me up, I kept my mouth shut.

I was the coward of all cowards and a terrible human being, but I didn't care. Not if it meant I got to keep Jackson all to myself for just a little while longer.

CHAPTER 2

JACKSON

I had a strict but simple policy when it came to Travis Rush.
Hands off.
I wasn't always successful in following my own rules when it came to physical contact with the younger, gorgeous cowboy, especially when he hurt himself or acted out because of some demon from his past that was haunting him, but for the times that I did fail, I had a pretty decent backup plan.
I got drunk.
Stupidly drunk.
That would definitely have to be the plan for tonight. Granted, I'd have to stay sober long enough to make sure Travis left the bar in one piece with the flavor of the week, or even just to get myself home in the rare case that Travis deemed the girl worthy of spending the night with. Most nights, I would've just spent the evening at the bar slowly nursing a drink or two while I pretended to enjoy the company of whatever woman hadn't been fortunate enough to find herself a date for the evening. With Eden being as small as it was, the ratio of men to women was pretty big, so more often than not it would just be me and Bull, the bar's owner/bouncer/bartender chatting about our kids, which I was entirely thankful for.

Tonight, though, I was definitely going to be indulging in a bottle of scotch when I got home and hopefully sleep through the moment Travis returned to the ranch with a satisfied smile on his mouth because Brandy Jarvison had finally given it up to him.

The sound of Travis tapping his fingers against the steering wheel momentarily distracted me from my thoughts of the evening to come. He'd been acting strangely ever since he'd come to my room and even more so after we'd left the ranch.

Our routine was common enough that by now he was usually talking excitedly to me about all the women we were going to bag. I never bothered correcting him that the only one doing any bagging was him, mostly because then I'd have to endure his attempts to find me a date for the evening. I was glad that at least *that* part wasn't something it looked like I'd have to deal with tonight. But I didn't like seeing Travis so anxious.

I couldn't help but glance at his bandaged hand and wonder what had caused him to lash out like he had. It wasn't unheard of for Travis to be a hothead around other people, especially when he felt like he had to compete with someone he thought was better than him, but for him to put a hole in my wall for absolutely no reason made no sense whatsoever.

On top of that, he hadn't spoken a word to me since we'd left.

Travis Rush and I were as different as night and day, and yet somehow we'd managed a friendship unlike any I'd ever had before. He was younger than me by about ten years and there were plenty of times when he'd act his age and just let loose and have fun. But he was also one of the hardest workers I'd ever known. Not to mention he had a protective streak that ran a mile long.

While he wasn't too much taller than me, he'd come from the deep end of the generous gene pool whereas I was still in the shallows... hell, I was still on the damn shore.

Travis was the quintessential, good-looking all-American kid with blond hair and blue eyes. He hadn't grown up in Eden so I'd never seen him around when he'd been a kid, but when I'd first met him, I'd figured him as the kind of guy who'd played football in high school and had dated the captain of the cheerleading squad.

Sadly, the reality of his childhood had been considerably different. Whereas I'd been the only child of a doting minister and his wife, Travis had been one of nearly a dozen mouths to feed and had grown up dirt poor with an alcoholic father and absent mother. By the time he'd hit his teens, he'd been in foster care. He'd run away from his foster home when he'd been sixteen.

Travis, of course, had brushed off his past as nothing and had talked about the physical abuse he'd suffered as just a normal part of his childhood that he was already "over." But it hadn't taken a genius to know that the internal scars he carried ran much deeper than the physical ones I'd only seen glimpses of.

"You okay?" I asked.

Travis's thumping stopped for only a moment. "Fine," he grunted before resuming his tapping. I stared at his profile and felt that familiar tug deep in my belly as I took in his good looks. As handsome as he was, he never failed to get me with anything simpler than his smile. In the years since we'd been friends, I'd made it my personal goal in life to make the man smile. Not one of the fake smiles he gave whatever girl he was trying to hook up with, but the bone-deep kind of smile that really meant something.

Silence filled the cab of the truck for several minutes until Travis suddenly said, "Hey, why don't we go fishing at your cabin next weekend?"

That familiar flip-flopping sensation began in my belly as heat crawled up the back of my neck. A couple of weeks earlier I would've given anything to have Travis to myself for the one weekend we had off a month. We'd gone to my cabin countless times and every time it made me feel like I didn't have to share him with anyone else. We'd even taken my son, Cameron, with us a few times. When we had, I'd silently pretended that we were more than just a couple of friends hanging out for a weekend. Maybe that was what had started all of this... that wish to have a family of my own like I'd once had. Well, not exactly like I'd had because my life with Jolene had been a lie from day one.

I'd been a lie from day one.

And it seemed like I'd have to continue the lie because I couldn't lose Travis like I'd lost Jolene. Granted, Jolene was still a big part of my life and she said she'd forgiven me for everything, but there was no denying that I'd taken more from her than I'd given. Fortunately, she'd found a man who was truly worthy of her.

At least I wasn't foolish enough to truly believe I could have anything with Travis beyond friendship. But besides my child, Travis was all I really had. As much as I wanted to change that, I knew that fate wouldn't come through for me on this one. Even if the ad in the Heart2Heart personals somehow reunited me with the guy I'd met in the hardware store, I was still reluctant to believe it would be anything more than a good time. Much like the many good times Travis had every time we went out.

But I'd take it. Now that I'd accepted that it would always be men I was physically drawn to instead of women, I knew the likelihood of having the kind of relationship that straight couples were automatically allotted was slim to none. It'd been wishful thinking when I'd mentioned maybe having more in the ad. At this point, I just wanted to know what it would be like to feel a man's hands on me, to revel in his touch, to bask in his praise. As much as my friendship with Travis meant to me, there was still a bone-deep level of loneliness that not even he could fill, at least not as my friend.

So lying to him really was my only choice.

"Um, I actually promised Cameron I'd take him to the zoo in Casper next weekend."

I turned my eyes away from Travis but swore I could feel him watching me. I wanted to call back my lie as soon as I'd spoken it. But I knew if I told Travis the truth, I'd lose him. Even if he could get past the fact that I'd been lying to him all these years about my sexuality, I doubted he'd be okay with it.

He'd never actually said anything against members of the LGBTQ community, but we lived in small-town Wyoming and were in a business where you had to be a man's man. I'd seen too many stories in the news about what happened to men and women like me who dared to go against the grain and stand up for themselves. While I admired their courage and silently rallied for them, I knew it wasn't something I'd ever be able to do.

"Cool," Travis said, his voice sounding strange. "I'll come with you. It's been a while since I've been to the zoo. Hell, I don't think I've ever even *been* to the zoo."

My mind raced with possibilities. For a brief moment, I found myself actually preferring the idea of going with Travis to the zoo with my kid instead of hooking up with some guy I'd only met for a few minutes in a hardware store. The reality was that the ad probably wouldn't even work. But at least I'd have the weekend to deal with the fallout and somehow get back on track with accepting that this was my life. Even if I wanted to go somewhere else where guys like me were allowed to be who we were, I had a son who I would never leave behind. That made Eden home for the foreseeable future.

"I, uh, think Jolene and Zander wanted to go. Make it like a family thing," I murmured. I realized as soon as I said the words that I'd fucked up because Travis went silent and in my periphery, I saw his entire body tense up. "Travis, that's not what I—" I began to say but he cut me off.

"It's fine," he bit out. "I understand. I'm sure Brandy will want to hang out anyway."

I tried to ignore the jealousy that ripped through me, because it was clear what he meant by hanging out, but the green-eyed monster would not be denied.

It took just a few more minutes to get to the bar, but it may as well have been hours. The second Travis pulled the truck to a stop in the crowded parking lot, he was out of the vehicle and yelling, "Catch you later," over his shoulder.

I watched him saunter into the bar, greeting men and women alike as if he hadn't seen them in years. It was another thing Travis did… he turned the charm to ultra-high to mask everything else he was feeling.

He wanted everyone to know he was just a good old country boy looking for a good time.

Only I knew differently.

I'd been attracted to Travis from the day I'd met him and if there'd been any lingering doubt that I was gay, he'd pretty much obliterated it. On the one hand, it had been painful to have to work so hard to hide my feelings from him day in and day out, but on the other, I'd also been able at least partly be myself around him.

I wasn't exactly a social butterfly and would rather spend time with the cattle I took care of than try to navigate a room full of people, but none of that had ever appeared to bother Travis. He'd seemed just as content as me to go fishing or take our horses out for a run rather than hang with the other ranch hands each night. The only exception was our weekly foray to the bar so that Travis could get his physical needs met.

Now as I watched him enter the bar with his arm around a girl who *wasn't* Brandy, I wondered what it would feel like to have him put his arm around me like that. Or better yet, what sensations I would feel if he were to join his fingers with mine.

It took me a few minutes to work up the courage to walk into the bar myself. People greeted me as I passed, but it wasn't with the enthusiasm that Travis seemed to naturally command. I couldn't help but wonder how many of these very people would turn on me if they knew the truth about who I really was.

I had reason to be afraid because while much of the country was slowly beginning to embrace the LGBTQ community, Eden was still years, maybe even decades behind when it came to accepting people like me.

I myself hadn't even really understood what I was until I'd been well into my late teens. But by then, I'd been convinced that the feelings I had were as unnatural and sinful as my father had always preached from his pulpit. I'd tried praying the gay away many times and maybe I'd even convinced myself that it'd worked for a while, but deep in my heart I'd believed what my father had taught his congregation—that although I was one of God's children, I'd turned my back on Him and His love and had chosen the path of the devil instead. I'd been so afraid of what would happen if the truth were to come out that I'd practically begged Jolene to marry me before we'd even graduated from high school. I'd done my best to be a proper husband to Jolene and a good father to our son, but with the truth chipping away at my very soul, it'd been Jolene who'd suffered.

Even after Jolene had ended the marriage, I still hadn't had the courage to pursue the needs of my body and mind. I'd been too afraid of losing my job, my son, and even possibly my life. Some of the very men I worked with had attacked a young man in town just a few months earlier because he'd dared to buy nail polish for himself. I hadn't seen the attack, but I'd heard about it afterwards and while the young man had been lucky to escape mostly unharmed, I had no doubt what would happen to me if the men I'd been toiling next to for years discovered my secret.

As I made my way farther into the bar, I searched for Travis. The place was jam-packed with people who were already feeling the alcohol they'd consumed. I got to the bar and signaled to Bull, who quickly brought me my usual—a club soda. I turned so I could watch the crowd for Travis while I sipped my drink. I couldn't quell the nagging sensation that I'd hurt him badly with my comments about my fictional outing with my son and ex being a family thing. The reality was that Travis had been a part of my family for a long time now, often spending holidays and birthdays with me, Jolene, Cameron and even Jolene's new guy, Zander.

I was in the midst of taking another sip of my club soda when I finally spied Travis's light hair. I stilled as I watched him snake his arm around a gorgeous blonde who was practically popping out of the upper half of her short dress. Jealousy twisted through my insides as Travis leaned in to say something to Brandy. The young woman acted like he'd said the funniest thing in the world, but I knew she was just using the opportunity to throw back her head so Travis could get a better look at her already half-naked chest. When Brandy straightened and fluttered her eyelashes at Travis, he took her hand and led her toward the back of the building where the restrooms were. I felt my stomach drop out as I realized what that meant. It wouldn't be the first time Travis got lucky in a bathroom stall, but somehow tonight was different. Maybe because I'd had my own chance to know what the touch of a man felt like and had blown it.

Hal, the man I'd met at the hardware store in Casper, had been flirting with me from the start, but it had taken me quite a while to figure it out. I supposed it was a mix of the natural insecurity I felt being around such a good-looking guy when I wasn't much to look at myself, along with the knowledge that some guys were brave enough to wear their sexuality on their sleeve, that had kept me from giving Hal my name and phone number when he'd asked for it. He'd stroked my arm a few times as we'd talked and while I'd felt sparks of sensation, it'd been nothing like what I always felt when I was around Travis. When Travis inadvertently brushed up against me, it wasn't sparks that ran up and down my arm; it was this strangely delicious red-hot fire that made my entire body come alive.

I'd put the ad in the Heart2Heart classifieds after I'd randomly come across the site. While I hadn't been expecting much to come of it, watching Travis now as he pushed Brandy against the wall and dropped his mouth to hers, I couldn't help but hope that maybe Hal *would* show up at my cabin next weekend. I knew that was the only way I'd probably ever act on my need to be with another man.

Even if it wasn't really the man I wanted…

As I watched Travis give Brandy the very thing I'd been wanting from the moment I'd met the man, I felt a little more of me die with each passing moment. I wanted to look away but at the same time I didn't. Even from where I was sitting, I could see that Travis knew how to kiss. Despite everything that was fake about Brandy, from her unnaturally perfect hair to her more than ample breasts, I doubted she could fake her response to the pleasure that Travis's mouth had to be giving her.

I finally managed to pull my eyes briefly away when Travis's hands began roaming over the curves of Brandy's body. It wasn't the first time I'd seen Travis with a woman, but for some reason it was different this time. It *always* hurt to see him with someone else, but to see him with someone who was the opposite of me in every possible way beyond the obvious made it feel like little shards of glass were shredding me from the inside out.

Try as I might, though, my eyes went back to the pair and I regretted it instantly because at that very moment, Travis pulled back from Brandy and took her hand again, then led her into the darkened hallway. I numbly turned back around to face the bar and as one image after another of Travis and his conquest assaulted my brain, I set my drink back on the worn countertop and pushed it away from me.

When Bull appeared in front of me, I didn't even give him the chance to say anything. "Jack and Coke," I said as I kept my eyes on the bar top.

"Ain't you driving?" Bull asked. If my throat hadn't been clogged with so many emotions that made me want to cry, I would've laughed. No one even saw me as Jackson Doyle anymore. I was the guy who drove Travis home after he had a good time. On really bad nights, I was the one the friend of Travis's date was stuck with until the pair were through with their hookup.

Fuck that. Maybe I wasn't the kind of guy who could just randomly hook up, but maybe that was because I'd never really had the chance. Maybe Hal from the hardware store would prove me wrong about myself. Any doubts I had about the ad I'd placed went up in smoke.

"Jack and Coke," I repeated, keeping my voice even and firm. I took the keys Travis had left in the ignition of his truck and slid them across the bar.

Fuck Travis, fuck Eden and fuck all of the small-minded people out there who thought the things I wanted were wrong.

I downed the drink that Bull slid across the bar to me and then asked for another. By the time the second one was warming my belly, I was able to drown out the imagined sounds of Travis moaning as he thrust his dick into a woman whose last name he probably didn't even know. By the fourth drink, my head was spinning but that was just fine with me because I could no longer hear Travis, could no longer feel his skin against mine, could no longer hear the laughter in his voice or the softness in it when he said my name... when he whispered it. No, all I could think about was that by the end of next weekend, hardware guy or no, I was going to know what it felt like to finally be wanted for exactly who I was.

Even if it was all just a lie.

CHAPTER 3

TRAVIS

"You seen Jackson?" I asked when I reached the bar. Bull was cleaning a glass with the little towel he normally kept slung over his shoulder. His eyes lifted briefly to mine.

"Have you?" Bull responded. He seemed pissed but I had no idea why. And I was way too agitated to care.

I was about to repeat the question when I felt fingers dust over the back of my neck. The touch was soft and light... *too soft and light*. Nausea swept through my belly as Brandy leaned in against my back and wrapped her arms around my waist like they belonged there. It was all I could do not to shove away from her.

"Come on Travis, let's go to my place," she whispered in my ear. Her lips skimmed my neck but instead of my dick leaping to life, it didn't even flinch. That reality had me pushing away from the overly made-up blonde.

"You seen Jackson or not?" I asked Bull again. I needed to get the fuck out of there. Jackson was usually waiting for me at the bar, but I hadn't seen him since I'd led Brandy to the bathrooms. Before that, I'd been completely and totally aware of him... too much so. I'd had to work hard not to be obvious as I'd watched him move through the crowd and then sit by the bar. The anger and rejection I'd been feeling after his comment about me not being family had grown into something more. Men and women alike had brushed up against him as he'd walked through the crowd or as they'd leaned against the bar to get their own drinks. Every single moment of contact, no matter how innocent it'd been, had had me fisting my hands but I hadn't understood why.

I still didn't.

The only thing I was certain of was that I needed to find Jackson and get the hell out of there.

Bull leaned almost menacingly across the bar, the muscles of his arms bulging against his T-shirt. His eyes flicked briefly to Brandy and then back to me. "Looks like you found what you were looking for," he muttered before sliding my car keys across the bar to me. "Jackson did too."

Before I could say anything else, he sauntered off to deal with a rowdy customer at the end of the bar. Brandy was still touching me, but whereas her touch had made me feel cold before, now I barely noticed it. What the hell had Bull meant?

"Come on, sugar," Brandy said as her hand slid down my groin. I actually closed my eyes in the hopes that my dick *would* respond to the contact but when there was nothing, I actually cursed out loud and grabbed her hand. It was a repeat of the humiliating show in the bathroom. My sure thing with Brandy had turned into a full-on disaster and I just wanted to get the hell out of there.

And find Jackson..

"I have to go," I ground out to Brandy.

I knew it was a foolish move considering what kind of damage she could do to my reputation if she decided to tell everyone what a complete failure I'd turned out to be in the bathroom, but at the moment I just didn't give a shit. I heard her calling for me as I walked away, but I ignored her and then found myself randomly asking people if they'd seen Jackson. Everybody said no and a couple of people asked if he'd even been there because they hadn't noticed him.

I wanted to punch those people in particular. How could they have not noticed him? Jackson was one of the kindest, sweetest men out there. And maybe he didn't have traditional good looks, but he had the most beautiful eyes I'd ever seen. They spoke volumes when his mouth wasn't able to. The man would give the shirt off his back to anyone who asked for it and he treated everyone like they were someone.

Even me.

I spent ten minutes searching the bar and parking lot for Jackson, but there was no sign of him. Bull's words came back to haunt me.

What had he meant by Jackson finding what he was looking for? Had Jackson hooked up with someone? Was he even at this very moment with some guy? The thought had me seeing red and before I realized what I was doing, I began checking all of the cars in the parking lot. I came across many couples taking advantage of the dark lot and privacy of their vehicles, but none were Jackson.

My mind raced with possibilities. There were a few motels in Eden where Jackson would've been able to find a measure of privacy with whatever piece of shit he was with. I told myself to leave it alone and go home, but as soon as I got back to my truck, all I could think about was some guy touching Jackson, leaning over him, putting his mouth on him...

I ended up slamming my closed fist on the hood of the vehicle and heard several people around me making comments as they walked past. Part of me kind of wished one of the men would take issue with me so I'd finally have someone to take my frustrations out on.

"Hey!" I heard someone call from behind me.

Finally, I thought to myself as I curled my fingers into my fist. It was the one Jackson had wrapped up for me and it was throbbing since I'd used it to hit my truck.

I turned to face whatever asshole had decided to confront me, but all the fight left my body when I saw who it was.

Mac, my boss at the ranch, was standing by his pickup truck a few spots over. His girlfriend was next to him. They both had disapproving looks on their faces and I felt like a little kid who'd gotten caught misbehaving.

Mac strode up to me, his sharp eyes scanning my hand and the small dent I'd managed to put into my truck.

"Problem here?" Mac asked. He was a big guy who commanded respect. Even if he hadn't been my boss, I would've felt the need to cower in front of him. He was more heavily built than me and had to be twenty years my senior. Despite being the owner of Broken Tree, he was always out in the thick of it working by our sides, no matter how dirty or backbreaking the work was. I respected the hell out of the man.

I shook my head and murmured, "No problem. I was just looking for Jackson before heading back to the ranch."

Mac looked around us and that was when I realized that several people were milling about. My eyes connected with Brandy who was standing by the entrance to the bar, her arms crossed and her glossy red lips pulled tight. She was definitely pissed.

"He left," Mac said. I felt like a bug on a slide as he studied me. My best bet was to thank him, get in my truck and go.

Of course, that wasn't what I did.

"Do you… do you know where he went?" I asked.

My boss eyed me for a long time before finally saying, "He was pretty drunk so Susan and I gave him a ride. To Jolene's house. For some reason, he didn't want to go back to the ranch."

There was no doubting that Mac believed *I* was the reason. That scared the hell out of me. What if Mac saw something that I was having trouble accepting? I needed to thank him and then go back into the bar with Brandy. I could still fix all this. But the idea of putting my hands on the woman made my mouth fill with a less than pleasant taste.

"Okay, thanks," I murmured, even as I glanced at my watch. It wasn't far to Jolene's house, but it was after one in the morning.

"Go home, Travis," Mac said. I wasn't sure if it was an order or suggestion, but it didn't matter either way. I went around to the driver's side of the truck and got in. I glanced up to see Mac returning to his date, but when he went to put his arm around her, she pulled away. If my thoughts hadn't been consumed with Jackson, I would've wondered what Mac was doing such a cold fish of a woman like Susan Carlisle. They'd been dating for at least a year, but I'd rarely seen them touch.

I tried not to think about Jackson or the ad I'd deleted as I drove back to the ranch. I knew I needed to come clean with him about what I'd done, but the idea that he'd just repost the thing and find the hardware store asshole was unacceptable to me. And that just made me feel like an even bigger dick.

I secretly hoped Jackson would be back at the ranch by the time I got there, but when I checked his room, it was exactly as he'd left it. I went back to my own room and tried to sleep, but it was a waste of time because every car door I heard slam shut outside had me getting up to check if it was Jackson. By morning I was practically dead on my feet, but the first thing I did was go to Jackson's room and knock on the door. But there was no response and when I opened it, the room was in the same state.

I spent the day doing my regular day off chores like laundry. When Jackson hadn't returned by the time night fell, I started to get antsy and tried to call him. But there was no answer. A call to Jolene proved no more fruitful, since all she did was say Jackson was busy. Jolene and I had always gotten along, but there was no mistaking the disappointment in her voice. She assured me Jackson would be back at the ranch the following day for work and then hung up on me.

But Jackson didn't return the following day, or the one after that. None of the other hands knew where he was and calls to Jolene went unanswered. I even went so far as to drive by her house, but there was no response to my knocks on the door. Once I got back to the ranch, I bypassed the house I shared with Jackson and the other hands and drove straight up to the main one.

I could hear raised voices coming from inside—Mac's voice and a woman's. I knew I should leave them alone since they were clearly in the midst of an argument, but my concern for Jackson was too great. I pounded my fist on the door and kept doing so until it was ripped open. Mac stood there, seemingly pissed, but strangely calm too. He was one of those guys who even when he was furious, you couldn't necessarily tell it. But I'd seen him beat the shit out of a hand once who'd been abusing one of the ranch horses. Mac was not a guy you wanted to mess with... *ever*.

"Where is he?" I asked. "He hasn't been home in three days and no one is answering at Jolene's house."

I expected Mac to rip me a new one for the interruption, but I was surprised when he drew in a breath and looked at me kind of sadly. "He asked for some time off. Said he needed to go to his cabin."

My stomach dropped out at the words. Jackson wasn't supposed to go to his cabin until the weekend. It was only Tuesday. Had he somehow gotten the ad back up? Had Hardware Guy responded? Were they even now together at the cabin?

"Sir, is there any way I can—" I began to say and then realized what I was asking for and what message the question could possibly send. People on the ranch knew that Jackson and I were friends, but my behavior was over the top. The right thing to say to Mac was to thank him for the information and then get my ass back to work. But that wasn't what I wanted.

"Make sure you're both back by Monday," was all Mac said and then he shut the door in my face. While the permission to take time off was a relief, the fact that Mac seemed to know something that even I didn't quite understand scared the shit out of me. But I also didn't hesitate to turn on my heel and hurry back to my room to get some stuff.

I was going after Jackson, but I didn't know why and I didn't know what would happen. But I did know that I needed to see him again so I could put an end to this thing once and for all. I'd get Jackson and myself back to where we'd been... to being friends. And then everything would get back to normal.

Yeah, normal... *that* was what I wanted.

Wasn't it?

CHAPTER 4

JACKSON

My heart was in my throat as I approached the front door of the cabin but it wasn't because I was eager to see who it was knocking on the other side. In fact, it was the opposite. I reminded myself of a couple of things as I forced one foot in front of the other. First off, it was Tuesday, not the weekend, so there was no way that Hal would arrive so soon. Secondly, there'd been no responses to my ad in my email so the chances that Hal had even seen it seemed unlikely. Third, and most importantly, I'd had enough time to realize that even if Hal somehow miraculously did show up, he wasn't the man I wanted... or needed.

I couldn't remember much about what had happened after I'd left the bar, but Jolene had managed to fill in a couple of the blank spots, including the fact that Mac and his girlfriend had been the ones to give me a ride to her house. When I'd gone to Mac to ask for some time off, he'd given it to me without question and it made me wonder what kinds of things I'd said to him. He'd also made an elusive comment about Travis being a dick.

He was right about that, of course. Travis was a dick. But he really wasn't.

Travis was just being Travis. The only claim I had on him was the one in my heart. And while I couldn't have claimed him publicly even if he'd been interested in me, *I* silently considered myself *his*.

Which meant I had no interest in giving myself to Hal or any other random stranger. If I couldn't have Travis, I didn't want anyone. I knew what a fool that made me and that I was condemning myself to a life of loneliness and heartbreak, but I couldn't pretend it was anything other than what it was. I was in love with Travis Rush and had been for a while. Just like I hadn't been able to turn off being gay, I couldn't turn off the feelings I had for the man.

I'd already decided that while I'd have to learn to live with those feelings, I didn't have to condemn myself to a lifetime of watching Travis with whatever bimbo he'd latched onto each weekend. I couldn't do that to myself. While I didn't want to lose Travis's friendship, there was just no way I could watch him build a life with someone who should have been me. That meant moving on without really moving on.

Okay, yeah, so I was technically running away. It wasn't a fact I was proud of, but I didn't see any other way out.

There were plenty of ranches in Eden looking for qualified help. Since I'd never leave Eden while my son was still living there, and coming out as gay wasn't an option or even really necessary since my heart had latched itself to Travis, I'd settled on loving Travis from afar. Once I got back to the ranch on Monday, I'd start putting feelers out for a new job. I hated the thought of leaving Broken Tree, but the idea of being so close to Travis and not being able to touch him was no longer a possibility.

I was done.

Just done.

I hadn't even quite made it to the door when it suddenly flew open and the man I'd been thinking nonstop about stormed into the cabin. I opened my mouth to speak but snapped it shut when I saw the darkness in Travis's eyes. It actually made me nervous. He looked like a man possessed. And yeah, it also kind of turned me on.

Travis's eyes held mine for the briefest of moments and then he was scanning the cabin. He strode past me and snapped, "Where is he?"

"Who?" I managed to ask. "Travis, what are you doing here?"

He didn't respond right away. Instead, he began looking through the few rooms that made up the cabin including the bathroom, the small bedroom and even the single closet near the front door. I could feel the anger radiating off him.

"Is he outside?" Travis asked as he ripped the front door open. "Where's his car?"

"What are you talking about?"

Travis stomped back into the cabin and slammed the door shut. I felt my stomach drop out when he flipped the lock on it. It was both menacing and another big turn on. I'd seen Travis get hot tempered before, but I'd never been the target of it. I knew in my gut that he would never hurt me though.

But that didn't stop me from stepping backwards when he approached me. My back hit the wall, leaving me nowhere to go as Travis came to a stop within inches of me. He looked haggard, like he hadn't slept in a while. I actually found myself reaching up to touch his face as I whispered, "Travis?"

He grabbed my hand before it could make contact with his cheek. But he didn't release it or push it away. All he did was hang onto my fingers and despite his anger, his touch was surprisingly gentle. My skin burned where he was touching me, but it was the best kind of burn.

"That fucker from the hardware store. Tell me he's not here, Jackson," Travis demanded, his voice soft but full of something that didn't quite sound like anger.

His actual words registered a second later. How the hell did he know about Hal? "What?" I choked out.

Travis's head dipped a little so that our faces were just inches apart. My stomach began doing somersaults. I wasn't sure if it was because Travis had somehow figured out my secret or if it was the fact that he was so close that all I would have to do was turn my head a little and I could finally get a taste of him.

"Tell me he's not here," Travis whispered. "Tell me that it's just you here. Tell me you left that bar without letting anyone touch you."

I couldn't make sense of what he was saying. Part of it may have been the fact that his thumb was rubbing over mine, causing flares of sensation to pop beneath my skin.

"What is this?" I asked, because it was beyond cruel. "Travis, what is this—"

"I deleted your ad."

This time I was sure I'd heard him wrong. I began shaking my head, but before I could say anything, Travis added, "I know I'm supposed to be sorry about that. I was… I was sorry. For maybe five minutes. But now I'm glad I did it because you deserve better than some piece of shit who picks you up in a goddamn hardware store. What does he really know about you? It's taken me years to see all the little things that make you so fucking special, Jackson. Sure, maybe he saw a smile, but if he hasn't seen you when you smile at your kid, then he hasn't seen anything. And maybe he was lucky enough to feel your touch, but he doesn't know the way you are with a new calf or foal and their mamas. He hasn't seen how you give your attention to whoever you're with one hundred percent. He can't know that you make them feel like they're the most important person in the world. He doesn't know what you sound like when you're nervous or tired, or happy. He has no fucking clue how you give every bit of yourself to your kid and your work and… me. So no, I'm not sorry I did it. If he'd wanted you badly enough, he never would've let you walk away without getting your number. If he'd known how perfect you are, he would've had his ass planted in front of this cabin every day, *all day*, since the moment you two met."

There were a million things going through my mind all at once, but I couldn't really process any of them. Travis was here and he was saying things to me that he shouldn't be saying unless…

I shook my head because that was one thing I wouldn't allow myself to believe. I pulled my hand free of his and put it on his chest because I was pissed. Pissed and just so fucking hurt.

"You are such a selfish asshole!" I snapped as I let my fingers bite into him. "I'm not one of your toys! You don't get to play with my feelings for you—"

That was all I got out before his mouth crashed down on mine. To say I hadn't been expecting the move was the understatement of the decade. Travis's fingers came up to clasp my face as he swallowed my gasp of surprise and then slipped his tongue into my mouth. All I could do was let out this painful whimper that felt like it had been lodged in my gut my entire life. I barely even got to enjoy the kiss because I began to cry. It was like that brief contact of his mouth on mine had lanced some kind of wound deep in my soul and all the rejection and denial and fear and helplessness I'd felt for most of my life began to bleed out of me.

I tried to choke back the sobs in my throat, but when Travis whispered, "Let it out, sweetheart" against my mouth, I completely lost it. My body began to shake violently and then my knees gave out. But Travis's arm snaked around my waist before I could fall. He pressed me back against the wall and eased one of his legs between mine to help support me. His free hand came up to rest on my cheek and he just held me as I cried. I wasn't sure how long it took before I was able to catch my breath and calm down, but the whole time that I was falling apart inside and desperately trying to rebuild myself, Travis kept repeating the same words to me. Apologies, encouragement, praise... and they were all there in the softest of whispers.

"Jackson," Travis began to say.

I shook my head. "He's not here. No one's here. No one touched me... no one has ever touched me like—" I couldn't get the last word out, but I suspected it didn't matter because Travis tightened his grip on me and his thumb stroked over my cheekbone.

"Please don't do this to me, Travis," I breathed. "Not you." I shook my head over and over again. I wasn't strong enough for any of this. I didn't understand half of what was going on but I knew if he kissed me again, that would be it. I'd never be able to come back from that. It wouldn't matter if I moved to a different ranch or to a different country. I'd never escape the hold Travis had on me.

Travis's grip on me didn't lessen in the slightest. In fact, if anything, it got tighter. His mouth was near my ear again and he whispered, "If I let you go, you'll run."

He was absolutely right. I didn't have the emotional strength to pull free of him, but if he let me go, I'd at least have a chance to get my grasp on reality back.

"Why are you doing this?" I asked.

I felt him shake his head against mine. "I don't know," he admitted. "I just know I can't lose you, Jackson."

Understanding dawned. "Travis, that thing I said about family... I didn't mean it. You'll always be a part of my family, mine and Jolene's. Cameron will always be in your life. He thinks of you as an uncle. That won't change. You'll never be alone. You'll—"

That was all I got out before his hand snaked up into my hair and he pulled my head back so that I was forced to look at him. "Is that what you think this is?" he asked harshly. "Do you think so little of me that I'd use your needs against you?"

There was no question what needs he was talking about, especially when he pressed his groin against mine. Despite my mind crumbling from the onslaught of emotion, my body was having no issue with making it clear what it wanted. My cock was so hard that it hurt.

"In case you haven't noticed, Jackson, you're not the only one needing something right now." Travis's voice was rough and uneven. But I didn't understand what he was talking about until he shifted his hips just so and his dick, *his very hard dick*, brushed mine through our clothing. Disbelief rattled around my already confused brain. No, there was just no way he was...

But he was. Travis was a talented guy, but I doubted even he could make his cock respond so completely to a body that was the exact opposite of what he wanted.

"I love your family, but they don't factor even one fucking bit into this," Travis continued. His lips grazed mine and then his thumb was at the corner of my mouth. "I don't understand any of this, Jackson, but when I saw the ad on your computer and I thought about some guy touching you like this"—his thumb grazed my lower lip and then his tongue came out to lick the spot— "I wanted to kill him. I had to settle for taking it out on your drywall."

I remembered the way Travis had punched his fist through my wall. The idea that he'd done it because he was jealous had the spark of hope that had sustained me for so long beginning to build and build in my belly. But my brain refused to let it take over.

"You're straight," I breathed against Travis's mouth. He was panting like crazy and I couldn't help but reach out my hand and rest it against his neck. His heart was going a mile a minute. It was another thing I knew there was no way he could fake. That stupid, silly hope surged.

"Uh huh," Travis murmured and then his mouth settled on mine. I forgot that he was agreeing with me that he was straight and opened my mouth to his. For someone who'd never likely been with another guy, Travis didn't hesitate to take control of my mouth, to own it. By the time he was finished with me, my entire body except for one important part was like a limp noodle.

I was trying to catch my breath and pretty much hanging onto Travis to keep myself upright when he said, "Jackson, do you think most straight guys can kiss another man like that?" He was pressing soft, sweet butterfly kisses all around my mouth. I gave up on trying to make sense of any of it and lost myself in every touch, every kiss. It was a good minute before I realized he was still waiting for response.

I wrapped my arms around his neck and threaded my fingers into his thick hair. My body felt warm and tingly and that little spark of hope grew bigger and bigger. But I had to remind myself he was still Travis. The same Travis who liked the flavor of the week.

"Maybe not so straight," I finally said. "I guess you've got a whole new world opened up to you now." I regretted the comment as soon as I made it because I hadn't managed to say it casually.

Travis leaned back and studied me. His fingers toyed with my hair and stroked down my face. He caressed the stubble on my cheek, then my jaw and I wondered if he was finally coming to terms with the fact that he'd been kissing a man. But his expression was soft and reverent and all the anxiety he'd been exhibiting when he arrived seemed to melt away. He rested his arm on the wall above my head so that he could lean into me again. His mouth was just millimeters from mine.

"The only world I want open to me is yours." I expected him to kiss me again, but instead, Travis pulled back so that our eyes met. "I didn't touch her, Jackson." I realized he was talking about Brandy and I felt my heart fall. But I didn't interrupt him. "Yeah, I kissed her, but I knew you were watching and I just…" He shook his head. "All this stuff was going through my mind, all these thoughts about you and they were so… unexpected. I didn't know what to do with them so I just, I tried to shut my brain off. I took her to the bathroom but as soon as I'd walked in the door, I knew I couldn't touch her. I didn't *want* to touch her. I told her I changed my mind. She thought I was joking, but I didn't care. All I wanted was to find you and go. Not because I expected you to be there waiting for me but because I needed you. Not anyone… *You*, Jackson. I needed *you*. I *need* you."

I wanted to believe him. I wanted to believe him so badly that I ached with it. I knew I should stop while I was ahead and take whatever I could get from him, but the thought of him regretting all of this tomorrow was like there was a knife being held against my heart. I wouldn't survive it if I gave him those last pieces of me and he cast them aside like they were nothing.

"Travis," I said as I began to shake my head.

"I don't know what's happening to me, but I know it's real. I feel things for you that I've never felt for anyone else before, Jackson. But I've refused to acknowledge them. Not because we're both men or any of that bullshit, but because I wasn't ready. My mom and dad claimed to have all these feelings for each other when I was little, but all it did was destroy them both… and us. What if that happened to me and you, Jackson—"

"It wouldn't," I responded before I realized what I was admitting to. I pulled in a breath and reminded myself that I couldn't make this about what I wanted. Not if Travis was doing it for the wrong reasons. "I won't leave, okay? You don't need to do all this to save our friendship. I—"

Travis kissed me hard and then his hands were roaming over my body. His touch was tentative, but he never once pulled back or hesitated, even when he reached my groin. As he stroked my erection through my jeans, he murmured, "You let all your friends do this to you, Jackson?"

I wondered if he actually expected a response. The best I could do was shake my head briefly even as I pushed my hips forward in the hopes of increasing the contact. Travis obliged me and began rubbing my shaft more firmly.

"Open your eyes and look at me," Travis commanded. I did so without hesitation. He paused his caresses as he said, "This. Is. Real. I don't know what label to put on it or what I'm supposed to call myself now, but I know that I've never wanted anyone more than I want you right now. *And* from the day we met. I see all those things in you that others are too blind to see. I know I've hurt you and I'm so sorry for that. Please just give me another chance. I don't want to lose you Jackson. *You*, not the friendship."

That little spark of hope became a full-on inferno as I gave up the fight. I believed him. I believed that he meant what he was saying.

"They'll never let us have this... this town," I whispered. "My son, Jolene... we can't put them through that."

He seemed to know what I was talking about and it was a comfort to realize that he'd given it some thought as well.

"We'll talk to Jolene together. And we'll figure out how to make this work without putting ourselves or our family in danger. We'll figure out a way to build a life together. Just say we'll try, Jackson."

I would do a hell of a lot more than try.

I would give him everything I had.

I told him so by pulling him down for a kiss. This time when his tongue met mine, I kissed him back. My uninhibited response seemed to trigger something in Travis because he groaned against my mouth and then he was pushing me harder against the wall. His hands were everywhere after that. Ripping at my shirt, sliding over my jeans-covered ass, and most importantly, rubbing my cock.

My hands were roaming as well, and I reveled in being able to explore Travis's body the way I'd always dreamed of. I loved the sound of his whimpers whenever I found a spot that was particularly sensitive. Our moves were awkward and unpracticed, but that only made what was flaring to life between us all the better. When I went for Travis's jeans and began opening his zipper, I pulled back enough so I could watch him carefully. He planted his hands above my head on the wall and watched me. Not my hands reaching for his cock, but my eyes. So I did the same and saw the things he likely saw in my own eyes.

Wants.

Needs.

Freedom.

Travis's hot, heavy cock throbbed in my hand as I pulled him out of his jeans. Travis closed his eyes in pleasure as I began stroking him. Fluid leaked from the head of his dick and coated my fingers, making the glides up and down his shaft easier.

"Christ, Jackson," Travis moaned and then his mouth was on mine. I would've been totally fine with bringing him to his release, but then his big hands were seeking out my dick and within a matter of seconds he had me free of my jeans too. After that, my brain shut down and it was all about my body.

Travis and I both fumbled awkwardly to figure out what the other liked, but it didn't take long before we were kissing and fucking one another's hands. I ended up coming first and when I cried out into Travis's mouth, he whispered my name and held me for a moment. His rough hand gave me only the briefest reprieve and then he was gripping both his cock and mine at the same time. It took just a few strokes of his own hand against my softening flesh to get him off. Hot liquid hit my belly where he'd opened my shirt and then some of it dripped down to mix with my own semen.

"Jackson," Travis murmured against my mouth several minutes later as we began to come down from our highs. "Promise me we'll try," he begged.

I shook my head, but when he tensed up against me, I grabbed his face and looked him straight in the eye. "We're not going to try. We're going to make it happen. No one's taking this from us, Travis. No one.

Do you hear me?" It was my turn to be firm and commanding. The relief on Travis's face made my heart swell. I gathered him into my arms as he nodded.

As we sank to the floor and just held onto one another, I knew I'd never let him go. I'd spent an entire lifetime searching for Travis and now that I'd finally found him, I'd spend the rest of my days fighting to keep him.

So, what if we had to hide a little longer? There *would* be a day where I could tell the world how much I loved the man in my arms.

Even if I had to make that day arrive myself.

*Want to see if **Jackson's ex**, **Jolene**, can find her own HEA with Eden's newest bad boy **Zander**? Choosing Fate is coming soon!*

WANT MORE OF EDEN?

Coming soon:
Choosing Fate (Jolene and Zander's story).

Available now:
Always Mine (Xavier and Brooks's story) Get it here.

Join my Facebook Fan Group: Sloane's Secret Sinners
Connect with me:
www.sloanekennedy.com
sloane@sloanekennedy.com

Subscribe to my newsletter for exclusive giveaways and content! You can get it here.

ABOUT THE AUTHOR

Dear Reader,

I hope you enjoyed Tempting Fate. Want to know how Jolene and Zander met? Check out their story, Choosing Fate now. And don't worry, you'll see more of Jackson and Travis in future Love in Eden stories!

    As an independent author, I am always grateful for feedback so if you have the time and desire, please leave a review, good or bad, so I can continue to find out what my readers like and don't like. You can also send me feedback via email at sloane@sloanekennedy.com

Join my Facebook Fan Group: Sloane's Secret Sinners

Connect with me:
www.sloanekennedy.com
sloane@sloanekennedy.com

ALSO BY SLOANE KENNEDY

(Note: Not all titles will be available on all retail sites)

The Escort Series
Gabriel's Rule (M/F)

Shane's Fall (M/F)

Logan's Need (M/M)

Barretti Security Series
Loving Vin (M/F)

Redeeming Rafe (M/M)

Saving Ren (M/M/M)

Freeing Zane (M/M)

Finding Series
Finding Home (M/M/M)

Finding Trust (M/M)

Finding Peace (M/M)

Finding Forgiveness (M/M)

Finding Hope (M/M/M)

Love in Eden
Always Mine (M/M)

Choosing Fate (M/F)

Pelican Bay Series
Locked in Silence (M/M)

Sanctuary Found (M/M)

The Truth Within (M/M)

The Protectors

Absolution (M/M/M)

Salvation (M/M)

Retribution (M/M)

Forsaken (M/M)

Vengeance (M/M/M)

A Protectors Family Christmas

Atonement (M/M)

Revelation (M/M)

Redemption (M/M)

Defiance (M/M)

Unexpected (M/M/M)

Shattered (M/M)

Unbroken (M/M)

Protecting Elliot: A Protectors Novella (M/M)

Discovering Daisy: A Protectors Novella (M/M/F)

Pretend You're Mine: A Protectors Short Story (M/M)

Non-Series

Four Ever (M/M/M/M)

Letting Go (M/F)

Short Stories

A Touch of Color

Catching Orion

Twist of Fate Series (co-writing with Lucy Lennox)

Lost and Found (M/M)

Safe and Sound (M/M)

Body and Soul (M/M)

Above and Beyond (M/M)

Crossover Books with Lucy Lennox

Made Mine: A Protectors/Made Marian Crossover (M/M)

The following titles are available in audiobook format with more on the way:

Locked in Silence

Sanctuary Found

The Truth Within

Absolution

Salvation

Retribution

Forsaken

Vengeance

A Protector's Family Christmas

Atonement

Revelation

Logan's Need

Redeeming Rafe

Saving Ren

Freeing Zane

Forsaken

Vengeance

Finding Home

Finding Trust

Finding Peace

Four Ever

Lost and Found

Safe and Sound

Body and Soul

Made Mine

Made in the USA
Columbia, SC
20 September 2022